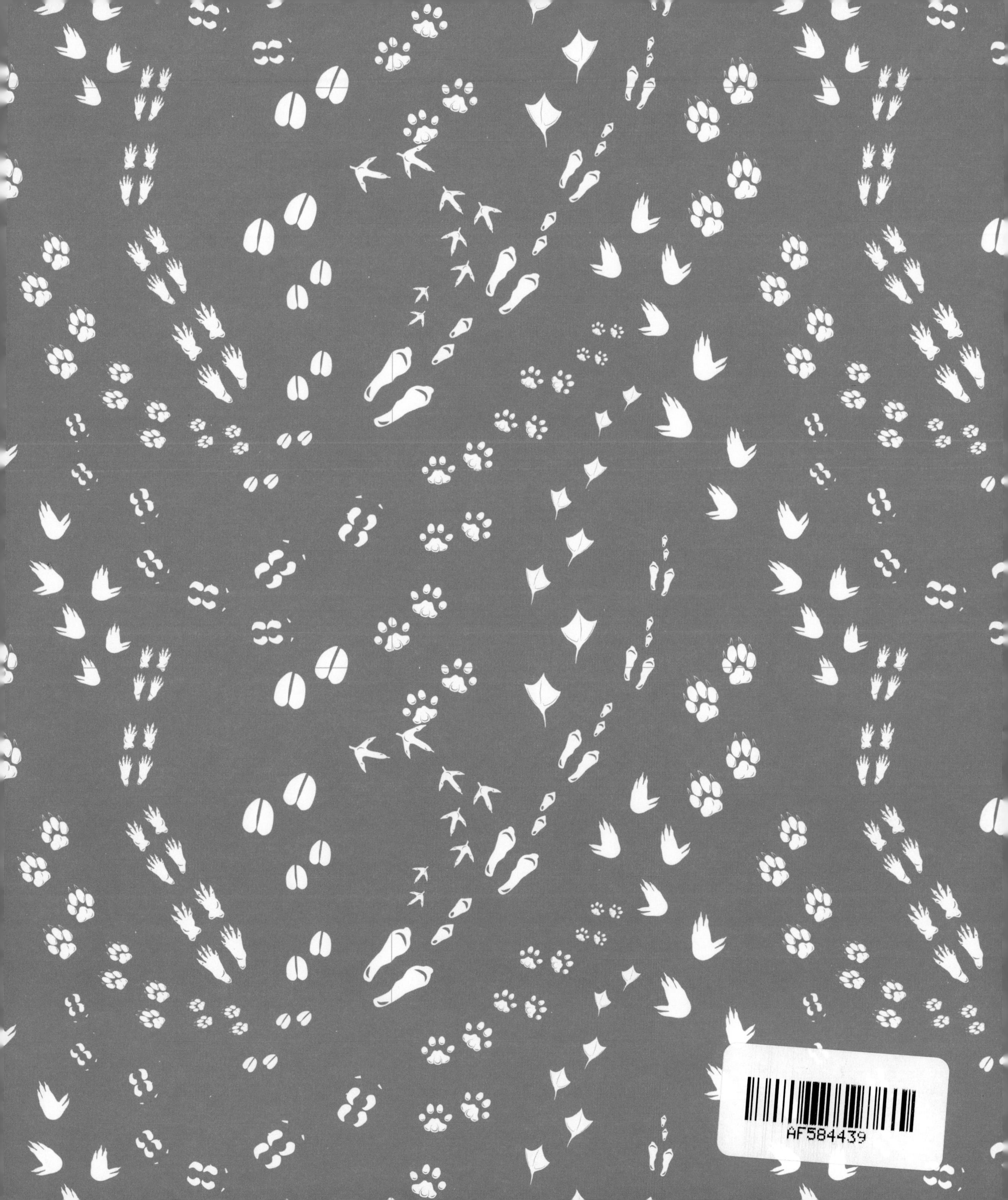

KOALAS DON'T RUN

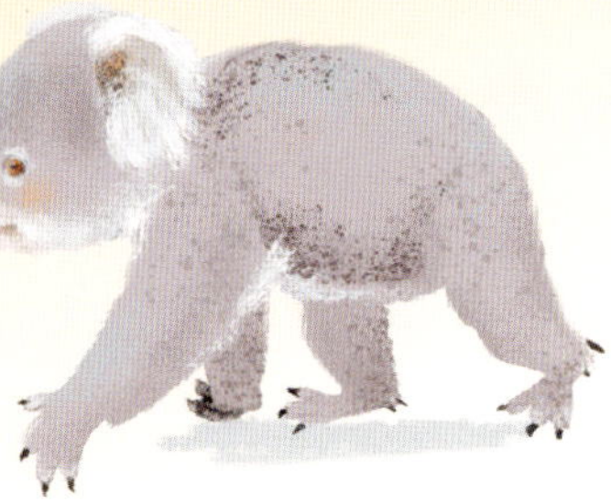

Janet White

REDBACK publishing

First Published 2021 by
Redback Publishing
PO Box 357 Frenchs Forest
NSW 2086
Australia

www.redbackpublishing.com
email: orders@redbackpublishing.com

ISBN: 978-1-922322-47-0
Author: Janet White
Illustrator: Janet White

Printed and bound in China.

NATIONAL LIBRARY OF AUSTRALIA

A catalogue record for this book is available from the National Library of Australia

KOALAS
DON'T
RUN
Janet White

Something was wrong.
Joey looked at the bright orange sky.

'Run, koala. Run!'

a cockatoo screeched as it landed
on the branch next to Joey.

The flapping and squawking
woke Joey's mother.

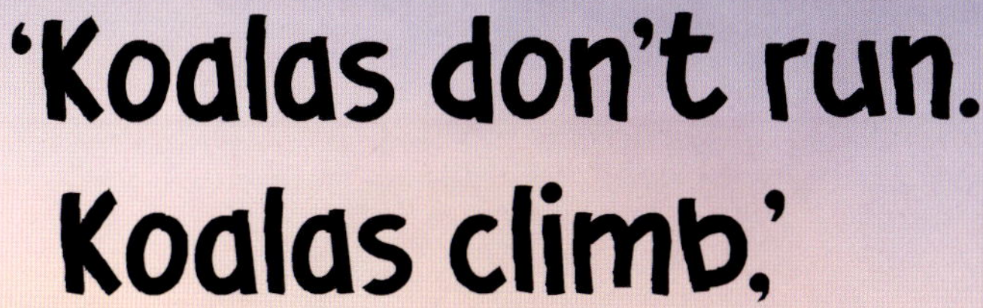

**'Koalas don't run.
Koalas climb,'**
mumbled Mother Koala.

Then she yawned
and fell back asleep.

Joey climbed up the gum tree
for a better look.

The clouds were blacker
than a cockatoo's feather.

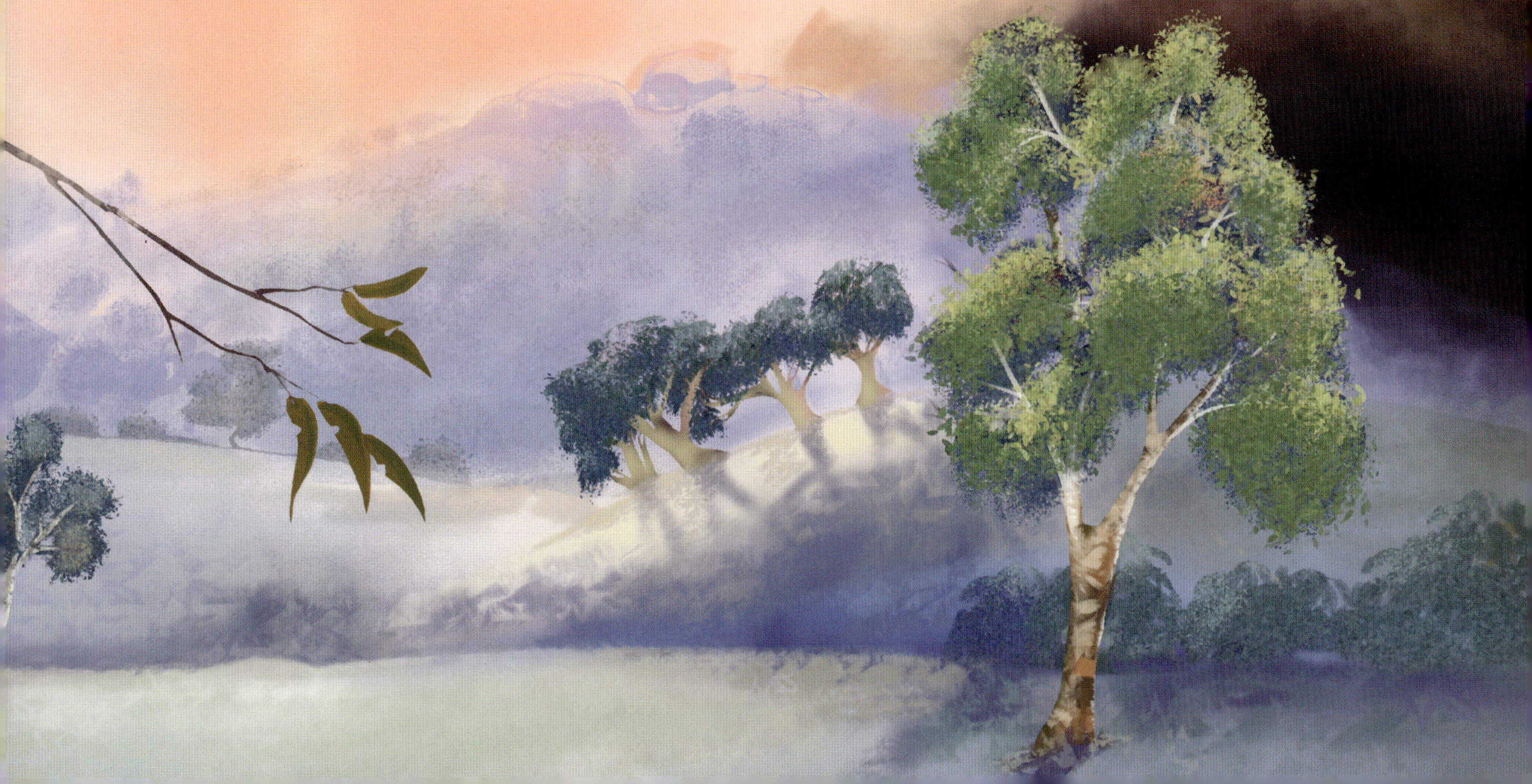

Joey wrinkled his nose.
Something smelt wrong.

'Smoke! Smoke!'

a flying fox called
as it flew past.

'Fly koala. Fly!'

it squealed.

'Koalas don't fly.
Koalas climb,' replied Joey.

As he climbed higher
he rubbed his sore eyes.

The smoke stung
even worse
than bat pee.

'Flee, koala. Flee!'

A green tree snake slithered past.
'Esscape to the ground and run as fasst as you can.'

'Koalas don't run. Koalas climb.'

Joey climbed higher.

Joey watched
gum leaves explode,
shooting out hot embers
that singed his fur.

'Bush fire!'

Mother Koala had woken up.

'Quick!

Jump onto my back, Joey.
We must...

…run!'

Mother Koala climbed down the tree
and **ran** as fast as she could.

She **ran** until
she could run no further,
then dropped
to the ground.

A dingo stopped
to sniff her.
'No time for tea
– I mean tears.
Jump onto my back,
young Joey.'
Joey clung to his mother's back until the dingo ran on.

A mob of kangaroos hopped by.

'I have room for one more.'

A kangaroo scooped Joey into her pouch.

Joey didn't want to leave his mother. He scrambled out of the doe's pouch and landed in the dirt.

His mother was nowhere to be seen.

Joey **tried** to run.

'Keep going!'

An emu pushed Joey along with his beak.

Joey ran as well
as he could.
He ran until he
could run no further.

Joey sat down.

'My paws are red.
My eyes are sore.
My fur is singed.
My throat is dry.
My home has burnt
and my food is all gone.
But worst of all...

...I have lost
my mum!

I am too tired to run
any further. Besides,' said Joey,

'Koalas don't run.
Koalas climb.'

Joey climbed up
the nearest tree
and fell asleep.

He had the strangest dream.

When Joey woke up
his paws had been bandaged.

His eyes were bright and
his fur was washed.

He had fresh water to drink
and gum leaves to eat.

But, best of all was when...

H_2O

...Joey saw his **mum**.

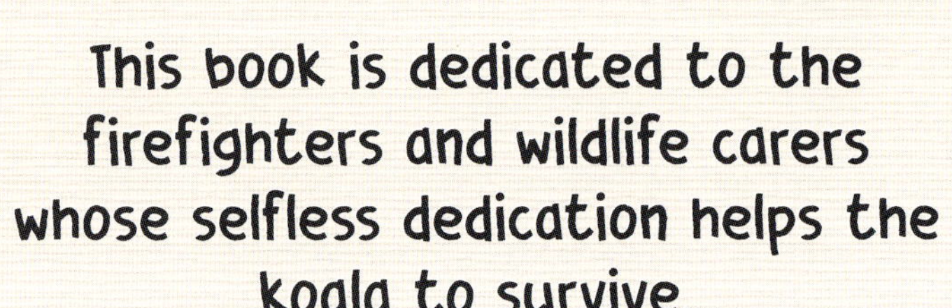

This book is dedicated to the firefighters and wildlife carers whose selfless dedication helps the koala to survive.

The world without the koala would be a very sad place.